Hello, Family Members,

Learning to read is one of the most important accomplishments of early childhood. **Hello Reader!** books are designed to help children become skilled readers who like to read. Beginning readers learn to read by remembering frequently used words like "the," "is," and "and"; by using phonics skills to decode new words; and by interpreting picture and text clues. These books provide both the stories children enjoy and the structure they need to read fluently and independently. Here are suggestions for helping your child *before*, *during*, and *after* reading:

Before

- Look at the cover and pictures and have your child predict what the story is about.
- Read the story to your child.
- Encourage your child to chime in with familiar words and phrases.
- Echo read with your child by reading a line first and having your child read it after you do.

During

- Have your child think about a word he or she does not recognize right away. Provide hints such as "Let's see if we know the sounds" and "Have we read other words like this one?"
- Encourage your child to use phonics skills to sound out new words.
- Provide the word for your child when more assistance is needed so that he or she does not struggle and the experience of reading with you is a positive one.
- Encourage your child to have fun by reading with a lot of expression . . . like an actor!

After

- Have your child keep lists of interesting and favorite words.
- Encourage your child to read the books over and over again. Have him or her read to brothers, sisters, grandparents, and even teddy bears. Repeated readings develop confidence in young readers.
- Talk about the stories. Ask and answer questions. Share ideas about the funniest and most interesting characters and events in the stories.

I do hope that you and your child enjoy this book.

— Francie Alexander
  Reading Specialist,
  Scholastic's Learning Ventures

To Ryan with love
—Aunt Gracie

For Amanda Paxton
—M.J.

Text copyright © 2000 by Grace Maccarone.
Illustrations copyright © 2000 by Meredith Johnson.
All rights reserved. Published by Scholastic Inc.
SCHOLASTIC, HELLO READER, CARTWHEEL BOOKS and associated logos are trademarks and/or registered trademarks of Scholastic Inc.

Library of Congress Cataloging-in-Publication Data

Maccarone,Grace.
  Mr. Rover takes over / by Grace Maccarone; illustrated by Meredith Johnson.
    p. cm. — (Hello reader! Level 1)
  "Cartwheel Books."
  Summary: One day in school, the class is taken over by Mr. Rover, who is very different from the regular teacher because he is a dog.
  ISBN 0-439-20057-1 (pb)
  [1.Substitute teachers — Fiction. 2. Teachers — Fiction. 3. Schools —Fiction. 4. Dogs—Fiction.] I. Johnson, Meredith, ill. II. Title. III. Series
PZ7.M1257 Mr 2000
[E] — dc21   99-462281
10 9 8 7 6 5 4   01 02 03 04

Printed in the U.S.A. 24
First printing, November 2000

MR. ROVER TAKES OVER

by Grace Maccarone
Illustrated by Meredith Johnson

Hello Reader!—Level 1

SCHOLASTIC INC.   Cartwheel ·B·O·O·K·S·®

New York Toronto London Auckland Sydney Mexico City New Delhi Hong Kong

"Mrs. Katz is sick,"
our principal said.

"You will have a new teacher just for today."

"Boo!" said the class.

We did not want a new teacher.
We wanted Mrs. Katz.

"You will like him,"
the principal said.
"His name is Rover—Mr. Rover."

Our class was surprised
that the teacher was a man.

But we were wrong.

Our new teacher was a dog.

It started out as a normal day.

We had spelling.

We had math.

Recess was fun.
Mr. Rover played catch with us.

He played tag with us.

He even played
basketball with us.

Mr. Rover barked to let us know that recess was over.

Some kids kept playing anyway.

Mr. Rover nipped their ankles. He herded them into the classroom.

But something bad
had happened.

Our class pet, Mousy,
was not in his cage!

"He is lost," said Penny.
"He will die," said Ben.

Some kids cried.

Mr. Rover barked.

He put his nose to the ground.

We put our noses to the ground.

He crawled out the door.

We crawled out the door.

He sniffed.

We sniffed.

We found Mousy!

Our class had fun when
Mr. Rover took over.

But we were happy when
Mrs. Katz came back.